CUENTO
DE LUZ

To Charles and Andrew.

- Erik Speyer -

Waterproof and tear resistant
Produced without water, without trees and without bleach
Saves 50% of energy compared to normal paper

Kubi Meets Rosita

Text © Erik Speyer
Illustrations © Erik Speyer
This edition © 2018 Cuento de Luz SL
Calle Claveles, 10 | Urb. Monteclaro | Pozuelo de Alarcón | 28223 | Madrid | Spain
www.cuentodeluz.com

ISBN: 978-84-16733-38-5

Printed in the PRC by Shanghai Chenxi Printing Co., Ltd. August 2018, print number 1668-8

KUBI

MEETS ROSITA

Erik Speyer

Kubi lived near a river with Charley, a tugboat captain.

The little dog loved watching the ships, the birds, and other animals from the bridge.

The Great Blue Heron was a special friend, along with turtles, ducks, and other water birds.

There was an antique shop right on the river where Kubi and his four-legged friends loved to play hide and seek.

When they got too tired to play, the dogs found cozy spots to curl up for a nap.

They enjoyed getting together to watch the big ships going up and down the river.

To cool off, the dogs jumped into the water with a big splash.

Kubi would often stop by the shipyards where the boat builders offered him snacks and a drink of water.

One day when Kubi got home, he met a dog who was new to the neighborhood. Her name was Rosita. She looked tired and hungry.

After Rosita had a rest, a snack, and a big drink
of cold water, Kubi and his friends gathered to hear
the story of her long journey.

Rosita was from a faraway town in the mountains. She had never had a real home, so she was often lonely, hungry, and frightened.

One day she got up the courage to leave the town and begin a journey to find a better place.

She hopped onto a brightly colored bus and headed North.

After the final bus station, she ended up walking for many days and nights through mountain valleys and jungles. It was very hard and she often felt lost and scared.

She had to cross a huge desert where she became
hot and thirsty.

Luckily a small bird, a Cactus Wren, showed her where to find water.

Rosita also met some friendly desert foxes who helped her find her way, although it was dark and scary.

The next morning, a kind man at a gas station gave her food and water.

Then she jumped into the back of an old truck
with a couple who were headed to a port city on
the mouth of a river.

And this is how Rosita came to meet Kubi. After hearing her story, all the dogs decided it was time for a swim. They jumped in the river to play with a baby manatee and its mother.

Later, Kubi introduced Rosita to one of his neighbors.
The man and his family loved her right away and gave her
a collar of her very own.

Kubi was tired after his exciting day. He went to sleep on the tugboat in the moonlight and dreamed of jungles, deserts, and other faraway places.